# The Reluctant President, Bellwether Bob

**Bellwether Bob, Volume 1**

Robert Alan Haviland

Published by Robert Alan Haviland, 2023.

This is a work of fiction. Similarities to real people, places, or events are entirely coincidental.

THE RELUCTANT PRESIDENT, BELLWETHER BOB

**First edition. June 6, 2023.**

Copyright © 2023 Robert Alan Haviland.

ISBN: 979-8223407706

Written by Robert Alan Haviland.

# Also by Robert Alan Haviland

**Bellwether Bob**
The Reluctant President, Bellwether Bob
Cruising with Mark Twain: Bellwether Bob
Cruising the Solar System: Bellwether Bob

# Table of Contents

*For Al and Betty Haviland,*

*loving parents.*

# Preface

This book is based strictly on fact, fiction, and fantasy. Any relation to any person, living or dead, maybe only coincidental. Some names have been changed to protect some of the guilty. No attention has been paid to the chronological order in the ensuing facts, fiction, or fantasy.

**THE AUTHOR**
**Anchorage, 2023**

# Chapter 1 — Life in Nome

It was another beautiful day in Nome, Alaska. After a week of minus 20 Fahrenheit, the day's high of minus 5 actually felt balmy. Noon was only a few minutes away, and Bob was anxiously waiting for the sunrise. He wasn't quite sure why— perhaps just to be sure that the sun was indeed in the sky before it set in four hours. Maybe because this was the holiday season and the Nome National Forest was beginning to grow and accumulate? (Every year, discarded Christmas trees are anchored into the Bering Sea ice.) This "National Forest" becomes part of the Bering Sea Ice Classic golf tournament every year. Green balls are used to make them easier to spot, and the greens are a small section of green carpet. Last year, Bob would have won the tournament, but hitting that polar bear gave him a three-stroke penalty.

Perhaps Bob was just feeling stagnated. Nome is beautiful, both winter and summer. The town is beautiful and unique. Located on the southern shore of the Seward Peninsula, the only access is by sea or air unless, of course, by dog sled in the winter. The local Inupiaq long used the area around Nome for hunting and gathering. However, the town itself did not exist until gold was discovered in 1899. The town blossomed with an influx of miners seeking their fortune. At its peak, about 20,000 people were living in Nome. However, today that number is around 3,500. That gold rush population of 20,000 included one Wyatt Earp of Tombstone, Arizona fame. Wyatt played it smart and opened a saloon instead of shoveling pay dirt. Yep, the first two-story saloon in Nome. The name of "Nome" itself had questionable origins. The most common is that it was a typographical error. A typographer many years ago didn't know the name of the area and wrote "? Name" on his chart. This was interpreted as "C Nome" or "Cape Nome." And so the name stuck.

Bob sipped his coffee, sitting by his favorite window at Fat Freddie's Restaurant. He was broken out of his reverie by a call from the door. It was Albert, his nephew. "Hey, Uncle! Still checking up on that sun?" Albert walked over and sat down opposite Bob. "Buy me a beer."

Bob retorted, "It's not even sunrise, and you want a beer? Plus, you're only 14."

Albert just sat there with his toothy smile. Now, Albert wasn't a nephew by blood. His grandmother raised him just like she raised Bob and his sister Felicitas after their parents passed away years ago. Bob and Felicitas referred to her as Aunt Mary. Mary Naami is an Inupiaq elder who carried on many of the old ways. She has a jovial personality and can always be seen in her floral design parka picking herbs, medicinal plants, and berries in the summer and fall on the tundra surrounding Nome.

Now, Bob and Felicitas, being adopted while very young, had asked Aunt Mary about their parents, and all Aunt Mary could tell them was that their parents were good people originally from Connecticut. Their mother was second-generation Irish. When Bob asked about their father's heritage, Aunt Mary said that all he ever said was "Yankee, Connecticut Yankee." Felicitas had asked her why her parents named her Felicitas. Aunt Mary always smiled and told the same story. Felicitas' mother had a 'difference of opinion' with the local priest in Connecticut. So, her mother wanted a name with Catholic roots, but one that she knew would not set well with her priest. When Bob asked Aunt Mary why he was named Bob, Aunt Mary just smiled.

Albert continued, "You're doing alright, Uncle. You do pretty good panning the beach for gold, and your comedy routine at the Board of Trade Saloon still packs them in. Your show is like a combination of those two old guys."

*Kids*, thought Bob, *there are only three ages: young, old, and real old.* "What are you talking about, Albert?"

"You know, that real old guy, Bob Newhart, and that guy on the Red Green Show."

"But there, there has to be something more," exclaims Bob. "I do make a little money with the gold, but that's hard work, and I'm not as young as you."

Trying to cheer Bob up, Albert continues. "Hey Uncle, you do have a good following on our YouTube channel. You wouldn't believe all the people from Greenland that watch you every week!"

"I have no idea why," replied Bob. "Actually, I, um, really have no idea what that, um, means."

Now Albert is a whiz with computers and the Internet. A few years ago, he started a YouTube channel featuring his uncle's comedy routine.

Bob bought Albert and himself lunch, and they chatted the hours away. Two o'clock came around, and the daylight was half gone. "Well, Albert, I think I'll head home and check on your grandmother."

"Okay, Uncle, I'll be along shortly. I want to check a few things out before your show tomorrow."

Bob shuffled to the door, threw on his heavy parka, turned to Albert, and said, "Well, um, okay, now, now, don't be too late." And with a wink, "Don't want the, um, polar bear to get you."

Bob shuffled along Front Street with the sun low in the sky, heading toward Aunt Mary's place. *Well,* he thought, *I am pretty lucky. Aunt Mary is a great cook; she took Felicitas and me in, and she has a wonderful, understanding, loving way about her.* Turning down a side street, he walked in the shadows until reaching home. Pushing open the door, he called out, "Aunt Mary, I, um, I'm home."

"So you are, dear. Come sit and tell me what's bothering you."

Bob thought, she always knows when something isn't quite right. "I don't know, Aunt Mary. It just seems like there's more I should be doing."

"Well dear, help me with dinner and tell me all about it."

So the two chatted back and forth like they'd done many times before. Finally, a short, uncomfortable stretch of silence. "Well, Bob, perhaps there's a change ahead for you. I see you traveling away from Nome, and this will change your life."

Now Bob was apprehensive. When Aunt Mary talked like this, it was almost like prophecy.

"What do you mean, Aunt Mary?"

"Dear, you will just have to wait and see. But I think it will help a lot of people."

Albert returned home and with that, they all sat down for dinner. As the dinner conversation went on, it was obvious that Albert was excited about recording and broadcasting Uncle Bob's show tomorrow night. And Bob still had to go over his notes for the show.

***

The following months passed as they always do in Nome. The sun stayed longer in the sky, the northern lights danced above them, the Iditarod Sled Dog Race came to Nome and ended under the burled arch on Front Street, and Bob did not win the Bering Sea Ice Classic. Bob almost forgot about Aunt Mary's premonition that travel was in the wind for him. That is, until one day, while at the Board of Trade, he bumped into an old friend, Will, from Little Diomede Island.

"Hey Bob, you still alive? I thought by now they would have found you frozen on the tundra!"

"Well, um, no, no, not yet."

Several years ago, while Will was visiting Nome, he and a few buddies got together and went "camping" (read "drinking") out on the tundra outside of Nome. Well, Bob had a little too much Jack Daniels and passed out. Being among friends, they dutifully covered him with a tarp before retiring to their warm sleeping bags.

"So, um, what brings you to the big city?"

Will just replied, "Ah, just some business and doctor checkup. Hey Bob, I hear you have a pretty good comedy routine going. Why don't you come out to Little Diomede and put on a show for us?"

"Well, um, I've never been out to the island."

"That's as good a reason as any to come, and we could use some professional entertainment."

Bob was thinking fast. He never really left Nome before, but Aunt Mary's words came to him. He was supposed to travel, and that would change his life. Was this what she meant?

"Will, I don't know..."

"Come on over and visit Bob. We can put you up and feed you while you're there."

"Okay, Will. Let's um, do it."

"Great, I'll make the arrangements. How about next week? You can just repeat any one of your shows from the Board of Trade."

***

So next week, Bob and Albert flew out to Little Diomede for a few days. Albert wanted to film the show and put it on YouTube as "filmed on location on Little Diomede Island in the middle of the Bering Strait."

The helicopter flight over was a little bumpy but generally uneventful. Will met them at the heliport. "How was the flight?"

Albert responded, "Great! And I got some good video to use in our show!"

While offloading the helicopter, another resident approached. "Hi! I'm Tony. Come to my place."

Bob shot a glance at Will and turned to Tony. "Um, ah, maybe later."

"Okay," replied Tony in a loud but friendly voice. Tony wandered away and, Bob being all loaded onto Will's four-wheeler and trailer, made the first of two trips to Will's place.

"You know," said Will when they reached his house, "Tony will never leave you alone until you visit."

"What, what, is the attraction at, at, his place?"

Will just said, "You'll see, and maybe there will be something for Albert's video."

After settling at Will's place, they took a short ride to the school where Bob's show would take place the following night. At the school was Tony. It was as if he knew they would show up. "Come to my place. We have coffee and seal and crab pupus."

Albert noticed the surprised look on his uncle's face and leaned over and whispered, "Uncle, pupu is the Hawaiian word for an appetizer."'How Tony knew what a pupu is, no one ventured a guess.

Will leaned over and said, "You might as well get this over with."

"Well, um, I guess we better go to Tony's."

So the caravan took off, leaving the school and heading to Tony's home and who knows what.

Arriving at Tony's, they dismounted the four-wheelers, and beaming like a proud youngster, he directed them into his home. A lovely woman met them and Tony introduced her as his wife, Sarah. "Sarah, we need coffee and pupus."

Sarah rolled her eyes and left for the kitchen calling out, "You might as well show them now, Tony."

Beaming, Tony ushered the party out the back door of his house. "Look! Look!" exclaimed Tony pointing to another island about two and a half miles away across the Bering Sea. "I can see Russia from my back door!" Sure enough, there was Big Diomede Island which is a part of Russia.

# Chapter 2 — Mr. Spamalot

Mr. Spamalot is a comic of some renown in the big city of Anchorage. He advertises his shows as "The Alaskan Shows the Department of Tourism would rather you did NOT see!" Well-known politicians have been known to make cameo appearances on his shows. Plus, he does his share to make Alaska the number one state for consumption of SPAM lunch meat (per capita basis, of course)!

As it so happens, Mr. Spamalot was in Nome collecting information for his shows when Bob was performing at The Board of Trade. Not that Mr. Spamalot knew Bob was performing. He hadn't even heard of Bob. Well, Bob's show was on Saturday and Mr. Spamalot arrived on Friday. After settling in at the Nugget Inn, Lot—as those in the know called him—wandered down Front Street to have a beer at The Board of Trade. As he stood in the doorway, letting his eyes adjust from the bright outside sunshine to the dim saloon interior, he heard from the bar, "Hooeee, and he's white too!"

By now, Lot's eyes had adjusted and he noticed three locals sitting at the bar, two ladies and one gent. "My type of place! Mr. bartender, buy the bar!"

Now buying the bar is an old Alaskan tradition, in which one person pays for everyone at the bar to have a drink. A good way to make friends, well, at least acquaintances, fast. One has to be able to take a quick survey of the bar and ensure there are not too many patrons, or it may be necessary to take out a second mortgage.

Lot wandered over to the bar and seated himself. Striking up a conversation with the three patrons and bartender, he learned that a local comic, Bob, would be performing tomorrow night.

"I'd like to see that show, but I have a photoshoot with a can of SPAM in Cape Prince of Wales. Might not get back in time to see the show."

The bartender, wiping down the bar, just said, "Well, try to make it. If you're late, we'll give you a discount on the ticket."

So Lot spent a few hours at The Board of Trade with a few beers and then wandered back to the Nugget.

The next day came bright and early, with sunrise at 4:20 a.m.—well, it seemed early after a sunset at 1:47 in the morning. Lot was off to catch his plane to Cape Prince of Wales.

***

Meanwhile, around noon, Albert was at The Board of Trade setting up to video his Uncle Bob's show that night. Bob was at Aunt Mary's rehearsing his lines for the show. It was hard to come up with new material every week for his shows. "Don't worry, dear," Aunt Mary told Bob, "I have a feeling tonight will be a special night for you." Of course, this didn't help Bob relax.

"What do you mean, Aunt Mary?"

"We'll just have to wait and see, dear."

Bob just shook his head and went back to his material.

The evening came and Bob did fine with his performance. Albert had a good video for his YouTube channel. Lot never made it back for the start of Bob's show. He made it back, cleaned up at his hotel, and made his way to The Board of Trade. Stepping into the saloon, he made his way to the empty bar just as Bob finished his show in the back room. All that Lot heard was Bob's closing line to his last joke of the show. "...and that's why the walrus crossed the road." And the crowd erupted into laughter and applause.

The crowd filtered out of the saloon, with some patrons hanging on to have a nightcap. As Bob made his way to the front, the bartender called out, "Bob, come over here and meet Mr. Spamalot." Now Lot had never heard of Bob, but Bob had heard about Mr. Spamalot. Bob hurried over to the bar, and the bartender made the introductions.

"What brings you to Nome, Mr. Spamalot?"

"Please, call me Lot. I came for a photoshoot with a can of SPAM in Cape Prince of Wales."

Now Bob knew about Spamalot's shows and SPAM. "But why Cape Prince of Wales?"

"Well, it is the westernmost inhabited place on the continent. I think it deserves a spot in the SPAM Hall of Fame. Plus, of the five most beautiful women I have had the delight to gaze upon, one was in Cape Prince of Wales."

"Well," Bob said, "I guess that's, uh, a good reason, as...as anything."

Bob and Lot sipped beer and chatted about Nome, Cape Prince of Wales, and comic routines. After a few beers, Lot leaned in and whispered, "Do you want to know the secret of being a successful comic?"

Bob leaned in and said, "Ah, yes, yes."

"Make people laugh!" roared Lot and leaned back. "I love this bar. Another round, Mr. Bartender! Look, Bob, you seem to have a good thing going here, but it's limited. Why don't you consider moving to Anchorage and trying your talents there? I might be able to work you into my shows as a warmup. But there are many bars in Anchorage that could use your talents."

"Well, I haven't really thought about that. It's a major move for me." And Aunt Mary's words about travel came to Bob's mind. "I'll, I'll think about it, Lot. It might just, just be a good move."

"Alright, alright, alright then, Bob. I'll see you in Anchorage! Check out this old bar on Muldoon Road. It's called The Cabin Tavern, and it's a nice local place. HA!"

# Chapter 3 — Move to the Big City of Anchorage

Over the next several days, Bob thought about what Lot had told him. Should he move to Anchorage? Would he be able to make a decent living? Where would he stay? Finally, he brought the subject up with Aunt Mary. She listened intently to his concerns. Finally, she spoke.

"Well, dearie, I think it would be a good move for you. But the question is, what do you think? What do you feel about a move? Remember, planes fly both ways. If it doesn't work out, you can always come back home. Plus, your sister and her family are in Anchorage."

"Yes. But I wouldn't want to stay with them, impose on them."

"Oh no, dearie. You wouldn't want to stay with them. They're a good family, but your nieces are a pair of hellions. I'm sure your sister can help you find a nice place to stay."

Felicitas had moved to Anchorage a number of years ago to attend the University of Alaska. While there, she met Bill, her future husband. Bill was a Captain in the Merchant Marines, having graduated from the Merchant Marine Academy in New York. They fell in love, married, and had two daughters. For some reason, Bob never visited them in Anchorage, although Felicitas and the girls had visited Nome quite a few times.

Bob felt a lot better after his talk with Aunt Mary, but he just couldn't make the leap. That is until the night he had that strange dream. Not that Bob put a lot of stock into dreams. He thought most were just brain-farts. However, this one night he had a dream that just stayed with him. In the dream, he was in his bedroom and a ghostly figure appeared. It had the appearance of Bob Newhart in a Jedi costume. Now Bob always enjoyed Newhart's shows, and although not a Star Wars fan, he grew up with Star Trek: The Original Series. So in his dream, Bob was a little perplexed about what was going on, and the ghostly figure also appeared to be a little perplexed.

"What's going on?" whispered Bob.

The ghostly Jedi replied, "I, I was hoping you would know, but, but I have this urge to kick you in your, your, ah, hind end."

Bob woke with a start and bolted upright. "Kick me in my hind end? What could that mean?"

***

When he finally tried to bring the dream up to Aunt Mary, she simply cut him off and said, "Dreams can only be interpreted by the dreamer, not by someone else. Take some quiet time and just let go."

So Bob did just that and decided he was going to the big city of Anchorage.

Bob called his sister in Anchorage and told her his plans. Felicitas asked him if he had a place to stay yet and Bob replied no. "Well, I have this friend Jed who owns an old house on the east side of Anchorage. No one lives there and he is looking for someone to stay there and keep an eye on it. He would probably give you a good deal on the rent."

"What's a good deal?" asked Bob.

"Well, I'll have to check with Jed to see if it is available and what rent he would take."

So Felicitas did just that and, in a few days, called Bob back. "Hey Bob, the place is available. It's a two-bedroom, one-bath house and Jed said he would rent it for $300 per month."

"That, that sounds reasonable. What's wrong with the place?"

"Well, it is an older house. I think it used to be part of a military housing unit that was bought and moved to its present location. You won't have close neighbors as it's on a double lot. Oh, and there are a couple of feral cats in the area, but as long as you don't feed them, there shouldn't be any problems."

So now Bob had a place to stay. He put his doubts aside and made the move. Since he hadn't met Jed or seen the little house, he decided to stay downtown Anchorage in the Marriott Hotel. On the second day there, his sister picked him up and drove to the little house to meet Jed. Jed appeared to be a friendly, helpful guy and was a retired construction contractor. After the meet and greet, they went into the little house. Yes, it was a two-bedroom, one-bath residence. But it looked like no one had lived there for twenty years.

"Ah, well, well, it looks a little rough," Bob commented.

"Well, we can fix that! I'll have the rug ripped out and a new one installed, repaint the interior, and have a cleaner go through top to bottom," replied Jed.

"That, that, would be...be great. No need for anything fancy. Just paint the floor battleship gray," said Bob.

"Okay, a cheap indoor-outdoor carpet, paint, and cleaning," responded Jed.

So the deal was set, and Jed said he would have it all completed in a couple of weeks. Bob thought that would give him some time to enjoy the Marriott and check out the venues for potential employment.

"Bob, will it just be you living here?" asked Jed.

Bob replied yes, although his nephew Albert from Nome may visit for part of the summer. Albert wanted to video some of Bob's shows and add "live from the big city of Anchorage." Jed thought this was great, and they all went their separate ways.

***

Back at the hotel, Bob sat and looked out his window. Having never been to Anchorage, he thought he had the best location to explore the city. The hotel had put him in room 1212, which Bob thought was a good omen as he was born on December 12th. His window was facing north, and he had a view of Mt. Susitna—or Sleeping Lady as it was called. He could also see the Knik Arm, the Hotel Captain Cook, Elmendorf

Air Force Base, and the Chugach Mountains to the east. Between the two towers of the Captain Cook, he could see Mt. Denali—McKinley. Also in the distance were the Talkeetna Mountains, which further north included the town of Talkeetna. According to Mr. Spamalot, Talkeetna is famous as a jumping-off place for mountaineers climbing Mt. Denali and as the town that killed President Harding.

Also visible from Bob's window on the street to the north was a place called La Mex. Having a Mexican restaurant in Nome, Bob appreciated the food and tequila. As it was late afternoon, Bob decided to walk to La Mex to check out their venue, food, and drink. After entering the restaurant and speaking with the hostess, he was seated and scanned the menu. "Uh, ah, I'll have the 1A menu item and a margarita blended with salt. And can I speak with the manager, please?"

"Okay, dear, one 1A and a blended Rita. The manager will be here shortly," replied the server.

After several minutes, the food and drink appeared, and a little later, the manager came to Bob's table. "What can I help you with? Is anything wrong?"

"Ah, no, no. I'm new in town and was...was wondering if you had a place for a comic in your venue."

The manager told Bob, "No, we don't have any comedy entertainers. You might want to check out the Hotel Captain Cook down the road. They do have entertainment."

Bob spent the rest of the day wandering around the city, playing tourist.

***

Now, although Anchorage is the largest city in Alaska, it is not large compared to many cities in the 'lower 48' states. Its current population is about 280,000. The second and third largest cities in Alaska are Fairbanks and Juneau. Founded in 1914, Anchorage was laid out by the military. Thus, most streets are either north-south or east-west. There is one road that sort of meanders northeast-southwest. This is Spenard Road, which, word has it, followed an old game trail many years ago. Spenard Road also happens to be where the Fly-By-Night Club was located and where Mr. Spamalot performed.

Downtown Anchorage runs from about 3rd Avenue south to 9th Avenue. South of this area is mid-town, and then South Anchorage. It wouldn't take very long to walk all of downtown Anchorage. Depending on the stops one makes, a few hours would suffice. It was in downtown Anchorage on 7th Avenue, where Bob was staying in the Marriott Hotel.

***

The next day after breakfast, Bob strolled over to the Hotel Captain Cook. After talking with the bellhop, Bob learned that the Whale's Tail lounge did have entertainment. Since it was still early morning, he didn't expect the lounge to be open. But he walked down the hall to see where it was located. To his surprise, the lounge was open and Bob walked in.

The bartender, a very attractive blond, looked up and said, "We're not open yet."

Bob, feeling confident, replied, "What, what about those two gentlemen at the bar?"

"Look, haole man, we are closed. Leave, or I'll call security," the pretty blond bartender replied.

Bob wasn't sure what a haole man was but thought this was not the time to ask, so he left, planning on returning later.

***

Later, late morning, Bob made his way back to the Whale's Tail. The pretty blond bartender was still there and a few customers were sitting at some of the tables, but the two older gentlemen were gone. Bob took a stool at the bar and waited for the pretty blond bartender.

When she finally came over to him, she stood there and crossed her arms, saying, "Are you going to behave?"

Now Bob had a few daydreams about this blond standing now in front of him. He knew she was out of his league, but...who knows? Obviously, Bob didn't know.

"Hey, close your mouth and order, haole man!"

"Ah, just, just, what does haole man mean?" replied Bob.

The pretty blond bartender rolled her eyes and looked at a man sitting on the other side of the bar. "Hey Anthony, get rid of this guy." Anthony let out a sigh and started to stand up.

"Wait, wait, I'll have a margarita blended with salt," blurted out Bob with an awkward half-smile.

"You'll have a margarita on the rocks, and if you behave, you'll have the salt," the pretty bartender retorted.

So in Bob's mind, he was making progress. Twice he was threatened with expulsion from the lounge, but here he sat with a drink on the way.

So Bob got his drink and he sipped the margarita for a while. Then he broached his next question. "You look familiar. Have we met before?" Bob asked with an attempt at a smile.

"I don't know, did I 86–throw you out of the bar—you before?" she replied.

"No, ah, no. Today is my first day here. I'm...I"m from Nome, first time in Anchorage," explained Bob.

"Well, that explains a lot," the pretty blond bartender replied, seeming to soften a little.

They chatted a bit and he asked if he could speak with the manager of the lounge. The bartender told him she was the manager and they were not hiring. Bob explained he was a comic and was looking for a venue. He found out that the Whale's Tail only engaged singers and musicians, not comics.

Bob stood up, getting ready to leave and asked, "ah, who, who were those two older gentlemen at the bar this morning?"

"They were the Governor; he owns this hotel, and Gordon."

Feeling a little more sure of himself, he asked the question that was on his mind all day. "Umm, just what does haole man mean?"

"Just go to Hawaii," she said with a slight smile.

# Chapter 4 — The Cabin Tavern

The next day, Bob had an early lunch with Jed at a place called The White Spot. It was a small café and one of Jed's favorites. Jed informed Bob that the renovations were coming along ahead of schedule and that the little house should be move-in ready in a couple of days. This was good as Bob's finances were running a little low. Jed graciously picked up the tab and again cautioned Bob against feeding the feral cats.

***

Having the whole day ahead of him, Bob decided to go on a long walk. The doctor had instructed Bob to walk more often. Looking toward the east, Bob saw the Chugach Mountains. Even though it was early July, there were still patches of snow on the mountains. Bob decided to walk in their direction and see what he could see. Traffic along the two-lane road was light. After a few miles, he came upon a crossroad and the sign called out "Muldoon Road." *Ah*, thought Bob, *that's where The Cabin Tavern is supposed to be.*

A few blocks down Muldoon, he spotted the tavern. It was a log structure with one end having a flat roof and the other a pitched roof, covered with sod, and a goat contently munching away on the roof. *Interesting*, thought Bob. The parking lot only had two vehicles in it, and on entering the tavern, it took Bob's eyes a few moments to adjust to the darker interior. He heard a woman's voice call out welcome. As his eyes adjusted, he saw the woman bartender, one patron at the bar, and an older gentleman at the end of the bar working at what appeared to be a newspaper crossword puzzle.

Bob took a seat a couple of stools from the young fellow at the bar, who he eventually learned was the man responsible for the maintenance and custodial work at the Tavern. Dave was his name, and he just got off shift. The older gent at the far end of the bar was the owner, Tiny.

Tiny had a grey beard and was dressed in a golf shirt, with reading glasses on a lanyard around his neck, and sat under a small lamp working on his puzzle. There was a sign over the door to the Cabin Tavern that said, "If you're over 6 feet, 7 inches, duck." That was for Tiny. Occasionally, a small, slight grin would appear on Tiny's face.

The bartender, Karen, was her name, Bob later found out, said, "I haven't seen you around. What's your story?"

Bob, distracted by her 'assets,' croaked out, "Ah, um, I'm new in town. Got in a while ago from Nome."

"Hey buddy, my eyes are up here!" Karen said, pointing to her eyes. And Tiny flashed that slight grin of his. "Are you going to order or what?"

"Um, yes, yes," replied Bob, correcting his gaze. "I usually drink beer or tequila, but I thought I'd try something different. What is a good Irish whiskey?"

"Bushmills Black is a good Irish," said Dave.

Karen lifted a bottle of Bushmills Black and said, "So Black Bush it is. How do you want it?"

Bob said straight, and Karen poured him his Black Bush into a small mason jar. They chatted a while, and Bob introduced himself and said that he had arrived in town from Nome a couple of weeks ago. He went on to tell of his comic act at the Board of Trade in Nome and that he was in Anchorage to see the big city and was looking for a venue.

Dave asked if he had any Irish blood, as he seemed to like the Black Bush. Bob replied a little, but not sure how much.

"Do you have Irish blood, Dave?" asked Bob.

"No, no. And I prefer beer."

Bob, feeling more confident—or maybe it was that Black Bush—turned to Karen and asked, "Do you have a little Irish in you?" Karen replied no. "Would you like a little Irish in you?" Bob didn't see Tiny flashing that grin of his.

"Do you want to be 86ed on your first day, Bucko?" Karen said. "AND MY EYES ARE UP HERE!"

"Ah, Bobby, Bobby, I hope you're a better comic than that line implies," Tiny said with that grin of his.

Bob assured Tiny he was and always had good reviews in Nome and even had a following in Greenland. This prompted Bob to explain about his nephew Albert and his YouTube channel, which, for some reason, the folks in Greenland seemed to enjoy. Finally, Bob asked Tiny if The Cabin might have a place for a comic routine.

"Bobby, we have live music every Friday and Saturday," replied Tiny. "I'll tell you what, if you want to try out your routine, you could be a warmup for the band, and we'll see how it goes over. No guarantees."

So Bob agreed and to start the following Friday.

Excited that he now had a place to live and potential employment, Bob went back to his hotel room and called his sister and Aunt Mary to tell them the news. Next, he started to prepare his routine for his opening night. He thought he'd start using the best of his Nome shows.

***

Moving day came and Bob was now living in the little house, as Jed called it. The place was a little run down, but Jed did spruce it up a bit with the new carpet and paint. Plus, a cleaning service did come in and give the place a detailed cleaning. The feral cats were on the property and contrary to Jed's advice, Bob did leave some leftovers out for them. If a feral cat could survive the winters in Anchorage with temperatures averaging in the teens and occasionally dropping to the minus figures, Bob thought they should have a little help along the way. One older cat seemed to take a liking to Bob and actually grew a little fat with the handouts.

The little house had a wood deck of sorts just above ground level. This proved to be a good stage for Bob to rehearse his comedy routines, complete with a feral cat audience. To be honest, the cats were more interested in Bob's leftovers than his comedy.

The one older cat even allowed Bob to pet it when Bob came close. However, the other cats would sooner bite the hand that fed them. Bob learned not to get close to the other cats.

All in all, the little house wasn't a bad place to live. Being on a double lot, the neighbors weren't even visible during the summer when the foliage came out on the trees and bushes. Now and then, a moose would wander down the driveway and bed down in the front yard.

***

The big night came, and Bob was ready with his best stuff. Albert had arrived to stay with his uncle and had already set up his recording equipment for Bob's show. Felicitas and Bill were also in attendance. Tiny opened the night, explaining to the crowd that tonight they had a famous comic from Nome to act as a warmup before the band. Bob felt the pressure. This night just might make or break his Anchorage career.

Bob started his routine. The crowd seemed to be receptive, and he continued using many of the stories and jokes from Nome. The half-hour sped by, and it was time for his closing. That's when the pretty blond bartender from the Hotel Captain Cook walked in. All she caught of Bob's act was the closing punchline of his last joke, "...and that's why the walrus crossed the road." And the crowd broke out with cheers and applause.

Bob gathered his props and prepared to exit the stage while the band started to set up their equipment. As he was gathering his things, he noticed Tiny over on his usual stool, and he was talking with that pretty blond bartender from The Whale's Tail. For some reason, he felt a little uneasy, especially when he saw Tiny crack that little grin of his. Tiny looked up and motioned to Bob to come on over.

"Well, Bobby, the crowd enjoyed your act. We may have to make this an ongoing event. Oh, and by the way, I understand you met this little lady here."

"Ah, ah, yes. We've met," Bob managed to get out.

"For a new guy in town, you manage to get around," said Tiny with that grin of his.

"Hey, haole man, I hear you knocked them dead. I missed all of your act except the punch line of your last joke. What was the lead-up?"

Bob, with that awkward attempt at a smile, explained she'd just have to hire him for an act at her bar. To his surprise, she said to stop by the Whale's Tail, and they could chat about it.

So Bob left and headed home to the little house, wondering how Tiny knew the pretty blond bartender and if he had a chance to perform at the bar she managed.

Turning into the little house driveway, even though it was ten o'clock, he noticed that fat feral cat. It was like it knew when Bob was returning and was waiting for a handout. *Hmmm*, mused Bob, *what could it hurt to give it a little of his leftovers?*

# Chapter 5 — Trip to Talkeetna

The next day, Bob decided to make a visit to The Whale's Tail and speak with the pretty blonde bartender about a possible gig. He wasn't sure just what happened last night when he saw her and Tiny talking after his performance at the Cabin Tavern. However, two gigs are better than one and will help to meet expenses.

So after a late breakfast at the little house and dropping his leftovers for the fat feral cat, Bob drove down to the Hotel Captain Cook. It never occurred to Bob why one of the feral cats had put on so much weight since he was there, but the other cats remained lean and mean, hunting bugs and mice.

After parking, Bob wandered into the Whale's Tail. And the pretty blond bartender was there stocking the bar.

"Hey, haole man," she called from the bar. "We're not open yet."

"Oh, uh, okay," Bob managed to get out. "I'll come back later."

"Sit your okole down," she said as she poured Bob a cup of coffee.

Bob thought to himself that he was out of his element. Not only didn't he know what haole meant, but now there's this okole word. Well, he thought things still looked promising.

So Bob sipped his coffee while the pretty blond bartender stocked the bar, and they started out with small talk. The conversation drifted to his performance last night and her invite to come talk.

"So, you...you think there may be an opening here for my performances?"

She responded that they have a great duo that plays five nights a week called "Jeanie and Michael." Their songs were essentially entertaining folk songs about Alaska. She went on to say that Bob's routine may be a good warmup for their act. And if Bob wanted to give it a try, she could make it work.

"Wouldn't it be necessary to get, ah, the Governor's okay?" asked Bob.

"Look, haole man, I run this bar!"

So they reached an understanding, and she refilled Bob's coffee, which Bob took as a good sign. As they chatted, Bob noticed a picture behind the bar that looked like the bartender with three Rottweiler dogs. Bob inquired about the photo, and she said the Rotties were her "kids," and she kept them at her house. Bob replied that she probably doesn't have any trouble with prowlers. To which she replied no. But she recounted a time when there was a prowler in the neighborhood one night, and her neighbor called to her to let out her male Rottie because of the prowler. As her neighbor called 911, she let out her male, "Turbo," who ran off into the night. The police arrived shortly and all briefed him on what had happened. About that time, Turbo trotted up, all proud of himself. He stopped in front of the pretty blond bartender and spat out part of a man's calf. The officer picked up the piece and said his report would say he found it down the road.

Bob thought, *Note to Bob, do not try to surprise this woman at home.*

***

Bob headed back to the little house and felt things were looking up. He arrived and found nephew Albert videoing some of the feral cat kittens.

"Hey, Uncle, how's it going?"

Bob went on to say that things were looking up and he now had acts at two venues or at least a tryout. Albert said that was great and handed Bob a check for $5,000.

Bob, with a lost look on his face, replied, "What's this?"

Albert went on to explain that he had been getting advertisers for their YouTube channel and website, and this was the first payment for the last three months, plus the souvenirs and memorabilia he's been selling on their website.

"You're kidding, right? Is this real? We have a website?" Bob wasn't sure what all that meant but knew what $5,000 was.

Yes, explained Albert. It was all real, but there was no guarantee this was going to continue. Albert said that the jackets he was selling with the punchline, "... and that's why the walrus crossed the road," sold especially well in Greenland. Bob finally felt things were coming together and was glad he made the decision to move to Anchorage.

Bob gave Albert a cut of the profits for all his efforts and decided it might be time to take a mini-vacation. A trip to Talkeetna seemed in order. Bob wanted to see this town that had a reputation for killing President Harding.

Albert was due back in Nome to check on Aunt Mary, so Bob asked his sister Felicitas if her daughters would keep an eye on his place while he was gone. The plan was to take the Alaska Railroad to Talkeetna and stay at the Talkeetna Roadhouse for a few nights. Felicitas assured her brother that would be no problem.

*** 

So Bob left for Talkeetna, looking forward to a few days of exploration. His nieces decided to stay at the little house while their uncle was out of town. It was a win-win-win situation. Bob got to travel a bit and had someone to watch his place. Felicitas had a few days of quiet at home, and the girls, well...

"Hey sis, this place is awesome! It's party time! Did you bring the brownie mix?" asked the older sister.

"Sure did, plus the special ingredient," grinned the other. "I also brought some catnip for the cats. No reason we should be the only ones enjoying our staycation!"

So the girls moved into the little house, baked some brownies, and they and the cats enjoyed...

*** 

Now Talkeetna is a small town about 100 miles north of Anchorage. Main Street is only a few blocks long. Its population is about 500 but swells in the summer tourist season. Talkeetna is located at the confluence of three rivers. These are the Chulitna, Susitna[1], and Talkeetna[2]. Thus, it is very popular with tourists looking to hook into some salmon or grayling. Flightseeing, camping, and hiking are also popular. It is also a jumping-off point for those attempting to climb Mt. Denali—Mt. McKinley).

***

Bob rode the Alaska Railroad from Anchorage up to Talkeetna and checked into the Talkeetna Roadhouse. On his first day there, he walked around the town, which actually takes an hour or so, and set up a fishing trip with Mahay's Jet Boat Adventures.

After returning to the Roadhouse, he wandered into the bar and ordered a Black Bush Irish whiskey. The place was quiet, with only a couple of other patrons. He struck up a conversation with the bartender and told him about his life in Nome, Aunt Mary, his move to Anchorage, and his comic routine. He even asked the bartender if there would be any possibility of performing at the Roadhouse. However, the answer was no. Bob was just about to ask how Talkeetna killed President Harding when in burst a group of mountaineers just off of Mt. Denali. "Buy the bar," shouted one in the group, and the bartender was off mixing drinks for everyone.

The next day, Bob went with Mahay's on a jet boat fishing trip up the Susitna River. The boat only had three other guests, so there was plenty of room. Although the salmon weren't running, they were able to catch some graylings, which the guide cooked over an open fire on a sand

---

1. https://en.m.wikipedia.org/wiki/Susitna_River

2. https://en.m.wikipedia.org/wiki/Talkeetna_River

bar. Bob thoroughly enjoyed the day and thought to himself that things just couldn't get any better. And Bob was right; things couldn't get any better, but they were getting ready to take an unexpected turn.

After returning to the Roadhouse, Bob found the mountaineers still celebrating, and the crowd seemed to have grown. He found a seat at the bar just as someone rang the bell. Now, ringing the bell at a bar is the same as buying the bar. Soon, a drink of Black Bush appeared before Bob. The bell was rung many times that evening, including at least once by Bob. Around midnight, Bob thought it best to turn in, and he staggered his way up to his room.

The next day came too soon, and Bob managed to find his way down to the dining room. He heard a familiar voice call out.

"Bobby, Bobby, you look a little green around the gills." It was Tiny from the Cabin Tavern, with that little grin of his.

Bob explained about his Talkeetna trip, his fishing adventure, and the previous night's excesses. Tiny, for his part, was in Talkeetna for a little fishing and was due to leave later that day for Anchorage, wishing he could stay a couple of more days. Bob was ready to call it a day and head back to Anchorage, but his reservations weren't for two more days.

"Say, Bobby, how about we switch tickets, and you go back to Anchorage today, and I'll go back later with your ticket?" asked Tiny.

That sounded good to Bob, who, at this point, just wanted to get back to the little house and chill out on the deck and recover a little. Plus, he thought he was coming down with some type of cold or fever. So, they made the switch.

Tiny bid Bob farewell and went out to schedule a little more fishing for himself. On his way out, he called to Bob, "Bobby, check with the bartender. He has something that should help with your cold and that hangover of yours."

So Bob checked with the bartender, and the bartender pulled a strange bottle out from under the bar and poured Bob a rocks glass full of the greenish liquid.

"Nurse this, and it should help you feel better," the bartender said with a slight smile. "It always works for our regulars."

Bob did just that, and the rest of the day was a bit of a blur. He sort of remembers checking out of the Roadhouse and getting to the train station. The rest of the day was hazy, but he did remember getting back home to the little house.

# Chapter 6 — Running for Congress

Dragging himself into the little house, Bob noticed the warm sunshine on the deck, his favorite lawn chair with that fat feral cat on it, and some freshly baked brownies on the kitchen counter. Humm, he thought, his nieces must have been busy baking. He picked up the plate and made his way to the lawn chair. After shooing the cat off, he sat down in the sun and started munching, and munching, and munching on the brownies. The combination of that "cold remedy" in Talkeetna and the brownies had their effect, and Bob drifted off into a nice nap.

****

The nieces drove into the little house driveway and saw their uncle sleeping on the lawn chair with that fat feral cat on his lap.

"Hey Uncle," called out the older girl, "you're back early. Is everything okay?"

Bob said yes and that he came back early as he wasn't feeling that well. However, he felt fine now and wished he had stayed longer in Talkeetna. The girls invited him to their parents' place for dinner, as their Mom just happened to be preparing one of Bob's favorite dishes. It was near dinner time, so Bob accepted and the three of them left for Felicitas and Bill's home.

It had been a while since he had visited his sister and her husband, so it was good to catch up. The girls disappeared into their room and the grownups were left to converse about what was happening in their lives. As Felicitas finished her dinner preparation, Bill set the table.

Bill asked, "Bob, would you like a little Irish whiskey with dinner?"

"Sure, sure," replied Bob, not feeling any ill effects from his previous hangover.

Bob explained how after a little overindulgence, the bartender at the Talkeetna Roadhouse gave him a home remedy that totally eliminated the hangover effects. At that, Felicitas cautioned Bob about home remedies as one never knew what was in them.

Dinner was ready, and the girls came down and joined the family at the table. The conversation started out with family events and eventually drifted to politics. Elections were coming up, and Alaska's sole Congressman was up for reelection. Alaskans affectionately referred to their Congressman as "Uncle Vic, Congressman for all Alaska."

Felicitas asked, "Has anyone registered to run against Uncle Vic? I hope not. He's done a lot for Alaska."

This was true; Uncle Vic had helped the State a lot over his many terms in Congress. He was one of the more senior congressmen.

"Someone should run against him," added Bill.

One of the girls asked why, and Bill went on to explain that competition was a good thing. Although Uncle Vic had done a lot for Alaska in the past, he had fallen out of favor with the House of Representatives. Some people were calling him a "Road warrior."

"What does that mean, Dad?"

Bill explained that a "Road warrior" meant retired on active duty. In other words, he was there but not really doing his job.

Bill surprised everyone when he said, "Bob, you should run against Uncle Vic."

On hearing this, Bob snorted a little of the Irish whiskey he was sipping. "What, ah, what did you say?"

Now Bill never thought Bob would actually run. He liked Bob, but not his chosen lifestyle. Maybe the experience of actually running for office would wake him up. Bob, on the other hand, thought it might be a good idea in order to gather some information for his comic routines.

Bill went on, "You can be a bellwether, Bob. If no one runs against Uncle Vic, people won't have a choice, so why should they even go to the polls? If people disagree a little with Uncle Vic's performance, maybe you'll gather one or two percent of the vote. If people disagree a lot with Uncle Vic, maybe you'll get five or six percent of the vote. You can act as a barometer or bellwether that Uncle Vic can gauge his performance."

"But, but I'm a nonpartisan. I don't belong to either major political party..."

"All the better, Bob, or should I say Bellwether Bob?" Bill went on to encourage Bob, adding that he should go register soon as the closing date was fast approaching.

Bob thanked his sister for the wonderful dinner and said his goodbyes. On the way back to the little house, what his brother-in-law said kept running around in his head. Would he be actually contributing to the State of Alaska just by running for Congress, even if he had no chance of actually winning?

***

The next day Bob woke up and that question still ran around his mind as he prepared to go out and grab some breakfast. He drove off for a late breakfast at Kava's on Muldoon Road. Kava's was a local restaurant owned by a fellow from Hawaii. Always a friendly place with good food and lots of it for a reasonable price. Bob sat, and the server came over with a pot of coffee. "Howzit?"

"Um, ah, it's just exceptionally okay," replied Bob.

The server had a quizzical look on her face as she asked, "coffee?"

"Yes, please, and a, ah, menu."

The server left Bob with his coffee and the menu. After perusing the menu, he decided on the Loco Moco with a side of Portuguese Sausage. His meal came and Bob dug in. His thoughts kept coming back to what his sister's husband had said the night before.

*What I need*, thought Bob, *is a sign to help me decide if I should go ahead and register to run for Congress.*

Bob had no delusions about winning such a race, but maybe he could get some material for his comedy routine. If only he had some sort of sign.

Bob finished his meal and went out to his truck. *Hmm*, he thought, *it's only half past noon; what to do*? As his gaze looked down Muldoon, it hit him: he should go to The Cabin Tavern, sip on some Bushmills Black, and ponder his next move. He drove the few blocks down Muldoon and parked his truck. Only six other vehicles were in the parking lot, and two of them looked like they were left by patrons from the night before. Bob entered the Cabin and let his eyes adjust to the darker lighting.

"Hello Bob," called out Karen from behind the bar.

"Ah, hello Karen."

Bob's eyes were adjusting, and he saw Tiny working on his crossword puzzle in his spot at the end of the bar. The only other people in the bar were two African-American ladies at either end of one bar section where Bob usually sat. Bob made his way to his usual spot and stood a few paces in front of the bar stool. Karen was looking at him with raised eyebrows as if asking him what he wanted.

Bob called out, "Black Bush!" He didn't see Karen take a few steps back, or Tiny's grin, or how the two ladies suddenly stiffened their spines.

Bob, totally oblivious to everything, stepped up to his bar stool with that awkward grin of his. He looked left to one of the ladies and was met with her drink in his face. Taken aback, he looked to his right and was met with a slap in the face. The two ladies stomped out of the Cabin.

"Ah, Bobby, Bobby, you have a way with women," Tiny said with that grin on his face.

"Hmm, ah, Bushmills Black please," stammered Bob.

"Too late, Bucko, that should have been your first order," grinned Karen as she poured his drink.

Bob regained his composure, or was it the Irish whiskey? *Eureka*, he thought. *That was the sign I was looking for.* "I'm running for Congress!"

Karen responded with her raised eyebrows as if saying he was crazy.

Tiny just flashed another of his grins.

So Bob explained the whys and what-fors of his decision.

When he was through, Tiny wished him good luck and then BOUGHT Bob a drink. This was unheard of. Tiny, very, very rarely bought a customer a drink.

"I'll tell you what, Bobby, I'll even contribute a hundred dollars to your campaign fund."

"Umm, campaign fund?" stammered Bob.

Tiny just worked on his puzzle with that grin of his. Karen shook her head and said, "Bucko, you need money to run. It's obvious you need a little help. We'll put a donation can on the bar for your campaign."

So Bob had a few more Irish whiskeys and chatted with Karen and Tiny on his "campaign." Then he took a few breath mints and went down to register to run for Congress.

# Chapter 7 — The Interview

It was a slow news week, so Bob actually made the local news as the dark horse running against Uncle Vic. That surprised Bob, but not as much as when the local news channel contacted him to arrange for an interview. Keeping in mind that this whole running for Congress was just to act as a bellwether for the sitting Congressman and to gather some new material for his comedy routines, he accepted.

The news channel wanted to tape the interview at Bob's residence, and the date and time were set. The day came, and Bob placed a few chairs out on the deck of the little house. Everything was ready, and the herd of feral cats were about as if they knew something was up. Most of the cats were in the scrubs near the end of the lawn—if one could call it a lawn. However, the fat feral cat was in the sun at the end of the deck. Bob threw her a few leftover shrimp tails from the night before.

The news crew finally arrived and began to set up their equipment. Bob and the lead reporter chitchatted about the interview, the little house, why he was running for Congress, and the weather.

The interview started, and the cameras were rolling. Bob was relaxed and treated the whole thing as if he was performing before one of his audiences.

The first topic was a general background of Bob's life. He explained that he and his sister were born in Connecticut and went to Nome as young children with their parents. The reporter asked if he had any memories of Connecticut. The only thing Bob could remember, besides living with his parents, was the way his mother celebrated St. Patrick's Day.

"We always wore green on that day. And we always celebrated the 4th of July also."

After reflecting a bit, Bob added, "Well, there was a good friend of my father, I remember. His name was Rick, but I don't remember his last name. They did take off now and then on fishing trips, but I seem to recall they didn't do much catching. One time they floated down one of the local rivers just for the fun of it."

The next topic was Bob's life in Nome and how he ended up in Anchorage. Bob explained this briefly and suddenly noticed one of the reporter's crew off to the side approaching a feral cat.

"Ah, you, you may not want to..."

"Yeow!" cried out the staffer as she withdrew her hand.

"ah, do that; they're feral," said Bob.

"Tell us about Bob, the man. What did you do for fun? Does Bob have many friends in Nome?" the reporter asked.

Well, Bob thought for a moment and then said, "Yes, I do." Well, he wasn't a social butterfly, but the friends he had were close friends. For instance, Bob elaborated, "I have this friend from Little Diomede; his name is Will. One weekend, a few of my close friends decided to snow-machine out from Nome to my friend Tom's cabin on Red Shirt Lake. We got to the cabin around dusk and noticed some large bear tracks coming off the lake and up to the cabin. As we were unloading, a neighbor came by on his snow machine and told us he had never seen tracks this early in the year and they were huge. The tracks went up to the cabin; there were scratches on the door, a wood pile was knocked over, and the tracks continued to circle the outhouse. We had been out to the cabin a week before and threw some leftover spaghetti down the outhouse. I told Tom not to do that because it would attract bears. But he did anyway. So there we were in the cabin; it was now dark outside. We ate and drank some beer. Then nature called, and no one wanted to go to the outhouse. I try to forget the rest of that night.

"Anyway, a couple of days later, we got back in Nome. After cleaning up, I went down to Fat Freddie's for a bite to eat. When I entered, I saw Will and another good friend, Dennis, at one of the tables. I didn't notice the grins on their faces. They asked how the trip went, and I just burst out about this huge bear that was stalking us. And that Tom was out now buying a big bear gun to go get that bear. About that time, my nephew, Albert, came in with what looked like a picture frame in a cloth bag. I hadn't noticed the whole Fat Freddie's' crew was around our table. Will and Dennis pulled the frame out of the bag. It was a photo montage of Will and Dennis walking with what appeared to be wood bear feet tied to their boots. I just didn't follow what was happening, even as the crew slapped me on the back and went back to work. I looked at Will and Dennis and just said, 'You didn't.'

Will finally said, 'It took you long enough.'"

Bob explained that this was the greatest practical joke ever played on him and would eventually get them back, but hadn't yet. Bob continued with the rest of the story.

"What happened was, after Tom, myself, and our buddies took off for Red Shirt Lake that day, Will and Dennis flew out to Red Shirt Lake with Dennis' Taylorcraft on skis. They landed, strapped the wood bear feet on, why they had wood bear feet is another story, and proceeded to 'attack' the cabin."

Bob noticed the reporter's crew beginning to yawn and look around. Obviously, they couldn't appreciate life in Nome.

The next topic was why Bob was running for Congress and why he thought he was qualified. Bob explained he wanted to offer the people of Alaska an alternative if just to act as a bellwether or barometer for Uncle Vic. He didn't mention collecting material for a comedy routine. The reporter asked why he thought he was qualified. Bob responded that he graduated high school in Nome and had the required civic and government classes just like everyone else.

"And what were your grades?" interrupted the reporter.

"Ah, well, well, I don't actually remember. But I did pass and graduate," Bob said. "And I understand all freshmen attend Congressperson 101 classes," he said with his awkward smile.

The interview went on with the reporter asking questions and making comments. The fact that Bob was a registered voter as a nonpartisan came up, and Bob said yes, he was, and his civic teacher said she would come back and haunt me if I didn't register to vote. Nonpartisan because both the Democrats and Republicans torqued him off at times. At this, the reporter raised her eyebrows, and Bob went on. He explained that, in his view, the two-party system would be the downfall of the country. He explained a "no-party" system would better serve the country. NOT a one-party system, but NO party. Having a two-party system polarized the people and made it necessary for the two parties to pander to the extreme left and right. When asked how this would work, he went on. Anyone could run for office in a primary. If that person wins a minimum percentage of the vote, he or she would go onto the general election ballot. No party affiliations. The Congress would have to find a consensus without majority or minority leaders. Of course, for this to work, political donations would have to be limited to, say, $200. Political Action Committees would have to be banned. Bob felt himself on a roll, but he didn't see the looks the crew were giving each other or their slight grins. Bob paused a moment and then dove in deeper. There should be a minimum level of intelligence and education required to vote. A person with no knowledge of reality shouldn't be able to vote. Would we really want someone to vote, for instance, if they believe a little green man from Mars told them to vote a certain way? Of course, if that little green man was wearing a *Star Trek* uniform, that would be okay. At that point, Bob had to make sure that it was a joke, with that awkward grin of his. It might be nice, Bob mused, if there was a way to determine if people had the country's interest at heart over their own finances, but how could that be done? Bob agreed this would probably take some Constitutional amendments and probably never be done. Our best hope is to educate our young.

Bob caught the reporter stifling another yawn as she asked if Bob had anyone in mind for his staff if he was elected. Bob knew this was an empty question and that they were getting ready to make the interview a wrap.

"Ah, no, no, I'll probably keep the crew Uncle Vic has onboard."

With that, the reporter thanked Bob, and she and her crew departed. Bob thought that the interview wouldn't make it to the news, but he wasn't counting on it being another slow news week. He made the 5 o'clock and 6 o'clock news. What he didn't count on was his nephew Albert contacting the news station and getting permission to replay the interview on his—their?—YouTube channel.

# Chapter 8 — The Debate Debacle

At first, Uncle Vic was furious that a Nomeite would actually challenge him for Congress. After all, he's been the "Congressman for all Alaska" for over 40 years. Then he realized this might be some free publicity, and he could have some fun with it. As luck would have it, the League of Women Voters decided that a debate would be in order between Uncle Vic and Nomeite Bob, or Bellwether Bob as his supporters—drinking buddies—have labeled him. So the debate date was set and the two candidates prepared themselves. Uncle Vic didn't do any preparation other than have his campaign print up some additional "Vote for Uncle Vic" signs. Bob spent a lot of time rehearsing debate questions with his campaign crew—drinking buddies—at the Cabin Tavern.

One day when Bob entered the Cabin Tavern, he noticed Tiny in his usual spot. But instead of pouring over his daily crossword puzzle, he was speaking with another gentleman of slight build and dark hair. Karen, the bartender, didn't even ask what Bob wanted to drink but just poured him his Irish whisky. Tiny saw Bob enter and waved him over.

"Hey Bobby, come on over. There's someone I'd like you to meet. This is Bernie; he owns a nice martini bar downtown. He ran for Congress once himself and can share his experience. Plus, his lounge has a nice outdoor area which would be perfect for your campaign to watch the returns on election day," Tiny explained.

Now Bob wasn't planning on having a big event for election night. He wasn't even planning on a campaign crew, but he had one nonetheless. Bernie sat there with a big smile on his face and went into his experience running for Congress. Bob didn't want to act ungrateful to either Tiny or Bernie, but his mind wasn't really on the election. What was on his mind was if Bernie would be interested in Bob's comedy routine, but he kept that to himself.

Time passed and Bernie bought Bob a few drinks as they chatted, and Tiny went back to his puzzle. The regulars started to drift in and before he knew it, closing time came.

***

The League of Women Voters secured the Dena'ina Center for the debate. It was a large convention center not too far from the Marriott Hotel and a few blocks from Bernie's lounge. As far as the debate went, it was a slam-dunk for Uncle Vic. Having been in Congress for over 40 years, he knew his way around Washington, D.C. The only thing Bob could offer was a new face and a reputation for honesty. When Bob was questioned about some of the answers he gave to the local news channel, half the audience looked perplexed and the other half lost in thought.

The debate finally ended, and Bob thought he might have made a mistake in running for Congress. New material for his comic routine wasn't worth the stress. Although he thought Mr. Spamalot might get some inspiration. As he left the convention center and walked to his truck, he passed a coffee shop called The Dark Horse Cafe. Well, after that debate, so much for being a dark horse candidate. He stopped in to have one of those fancy coffees and just sat in the corner brooding. What the heck, he thought, might as well go have an Irish whiskey or two. Where to go, where to go? Bernie's lounge was just down the road a few blocks. But that pretty blond bartender at the Whale's Tail was just as far in the other direction. Bernie's, Whale's Tail, Bernie's, Whale's Tail...No question, and off Bob went to see the pretty blond bartender.

When he arrived, the bar was buzzing with commotion. Evidently, the bar had the debate on the television sets in the lounge.

"Hey, there he is! One of us true Alaskans! And an honest man to boot!" shouted one man at the bar. People came up to Bob to congratulate him and shake his hand. Bob was lost and stood there with that awkward half-smile of his, wondering what the heck was happening.

"Get that man a drink! Get him the best Irish whiskey in the house!" called out another.

What Bob didn't know was that the pretty blond bartender had been passing the hat for donations for Bob's campaign.

What Bob also didn't know until later was that Uncle Vic was caught after the debate with a hot mic. He made some disparaging remarks about the people of Alaska, including "You wouldn't believe what they let me get away with," "I don't even have to show up in Congress, they pay me anyway," and "valley trash, the whole state is an ignorant trash pile." Who Uncle Vic was talking to at the time isn't known, but a whole lot of people began to look at the coming election with a new set of eyes.

Bob was a little awe-struck. He saw that pretty blond bartender motion him over to her. Of course, he thought she wanted to talk with him and approached with that hope.

"Hey, haole man," she called out, "there are a couple of people who want to speak with you."

With that, she introduced him to the Governor and Gordon. The Governor suggested they go up to his office as the noise was a bit overwhelming in the lounge. As they left, Bob looked back and saw that pretty blond bartender giving him a smile and a nod. They walked up one flight of stairs and entered the Governor's office.

Bob started the conversation with his typical awkwardness, "Ah, ah, Mr. Governor, wa, what can I do for you?"

"Well, young man," the Governor started out, "first, let me introduce you to my good friend here, Gordon. He and I go way back, and we both have something in common."

Bob could tell the Governor liked to spin a good story, and he listened intently. Maybe he'd gather some material for his comedy routine, as Bob still did not grasp what actually happened this night.

"Gordon and I used to be professional boxers, old-school boxers. In our day, we held our fists with the palm side facing up, not down like they do today. And our gloves weren't the heavily padded ones they use today."

Bob looked at Gordon and could tell he had received his share of punches to the face and ears.

"First of all, son, call me Wally," the Governor continued. Wally went on to tell Bob that he and Gordon had something else in common, and it was Irish roots. Although Gordon was full-on Irish, Bob was only about half Irish. Gordon said he wouldn't hold that against him, especially considering his taste for good Irish whiskey. And Bob wondered how the Governor knew about Bob's background.

The Governor went on to say that he always has a morning coffee in The Whale's Tail and has a good conversation with the bartender on the goings-on in the hotel and the city.

"I've been checking up on you, son, and I like what I see," the Governor continued. "We need fresh blood in Washington. Believe me, I know. I spent time there, and the politics are stifling. We need a local boy we can count on."

And Gordon was nodding with tight lips as the Governor spoke.

As the conversation continued, Bob indicated he never thought he would get this far, especially after his poor performance at the debate. The Governor said not to worry; with his experience and coaching, Bob would do fine.

"Well, son," continued the Governor, "we'll get together again and plan on some campaign advertising. For now, get back to The Whale's Tail and celebrate with your friends."

So off went Bellwether Bob back to the lounge. On entering, he received another round of cheers and another round of Irish whiskey. He also received a knowing smile from that pretty blond bartender.

# Chapter 9 — Election Day

Bob had no recollection of how he got home that night of the debate. He vaguely remembered speaking with the Governor, too many Irish whiskeys, and the pretty blond bartender's smile. But here he was, home and in his own bed. Maybe the bartender brought him home and put him to bed? The smile on his face disappeared into a look of puzzlement when he looked over and there, sleeping in a cot, was his nephew Albert. Then he smelled some bacon, eggs, and coffee.

"Come on, you lazy heads, time for breakfast!" a familiar voice called out from the kitchen. As soon as his head cleared a little more, he looked at Albert and realized it was Aunt Mary calling from the kitchen.

Bob and Albert dressed and moved into the dining area where breakfast had been set.

"It's about time," Aunt Mary said as she poured them both a cup of hot coffee. "I hear you had quite a night last night. Just what happened?" she asked with that smile of hers.

So Bob brought both Aunt Mary and Albert up to date, explaining he still didn't quite know what or how he ended up as a contender for Congressman. With that, Aunt Mary reminded him of what she said long ago about a trip and helping people.

It turns out that Aunt Mary and Albert had decided to visit Bob in Anchorage before the debate had been scheduled. They arrived on the day of the debate and went to Bob's house, but of course, he wasn't there. So Aunt Mary called Tiny—Bob had no idea how they knew each other—-and found out where Bob was. Unknown to Bob, they were in the audience for the debate but were unable to get to him after the debate when Bob left for the Dark Horse Cafe and The Whale's Tail.

And as it worked out, Albert got permission to rebroadcast the debate, including the hot mic episode, on his YouTube channel, much to Bob's surprise and slight embarrassment.

***

Whether it was Bob's naiveté, honesty, the hot mic incident, or Albert's YouTube channel, Bob started to rise in the polls. Uncle Vic was furious and spent most of his campaign funds on television ads telling how great he was and how stupid Bob was. This didn't sit well with Alaskans. Oh, and Uncle Vic also spent some campaign funds brainstorming election strategy... at a dude hunting ranch in Texas.

Election day was fast approaching. Bernie gracefully offered his lounge for a fund-raising party and as Bob's headquarters to watch the returns come in.

Bob arrived at Bernie's and saw the place was packed. A band was playing on the outdoor stage, and the servers were bringing out food and drink to the crowd. Bernie came over to Bob with that bright, friendly smile of his and shook Bob's hand.

"Mr. Congressman, welcome to my humble establishment," Bernie said, pumping Bob's hand up and down. "Make yourself at home, and everything for you is on me. Food and drink."

Bob mumbled his thanks and said that it was a little early and probably improbable to be a Congressman.

Bob found one of Bernie's Big Mouth Beef Burgers and a glass of Irish whiskey in his hands. As he made the rounds, he thought it was such a beautiful day. The sun was shining, and friendly people were all around. The Governor and Gordon, Tiny, and bartender Karen were there also. He spotted Aunt Mary, who gave him a knowing nod, and Albert, who was videoing for his YouTube channel, no doubt. And the pretty blond bartender was there also! Bob made his way over to her, and she just smiled. After a few moments of awkward silence, Bob managed to blurt out hi.

"Already haole man? You should learn how to pace yourself," she responded.

"Ah, ah, no, no. I meant hello," Bob mumbled.

The pretty blond bartender just smiled, and Bob relaxed a bit. They talked a little while. Bob tried to eat his burger and drink his whiskey without slopping the burger on himself or spilling his drink.

When he asked what she was drinking, she responded, "A martini, haole man. This IS a martini bar."

***

The countdown to election day was mildly entertaining. Uncle Vic continued his diatribe about how great he was and how ignorant Bob was. He dug up some not-so-flattering stories about Bob and made sure they made it into the election campaign ads on TV. One had to do with a hike on the fishing trip that Bob and his good friend Tom went on a while back. Evidently, it was a rather long hike in, and when they arrived, they were all hot and tired. They dropped their rucksacks, collapsed on the ground, and caught their breath. Tom eventually turned to Bob and asked if he would like a cold beer. Bob asked if Tom actually packed in beer for the trip. At which Tom gave a slight laugh and said with a chuckle, "No, but you did. A six-pack with ice. You left your pack unattended before we left, and I knew you would appreciate a cold beer. So I just added it to your load."

Another story that made it to the political ads financed by Uncle Vic was a story about a hovercraft. Again, years ago, Bob went in with a few of his buddies to purchase a used, four-person hovercraft. One week, Bob and co-owner Mark went on a moose hunt. After failing totally, they took one more run up the river. On the way back, the craft caught a tailwind and flipped completely over. The two of them scrambled onto the belly of the beast and took stock of their situation. The cage around the prop was at least seven feet from top to bottom of the craft, and it was grounded to a standstill. The water was cold, with pieces of glacial ice floating past. They were soaking wet, but fortunately, both were wearing wool. What was passing through both their minds was that they would have to get back into that cold water to get to shore. What the ad didn't mention was that Mark was originally from Texas and loved country music. Bob, growing up in Nome, didn't really like or dislike country music. But after this shared adventure, some sort of mental transference took place and Bob took to country music like a fish swimming upstream to spawn.

Now, these stories were supposed to show how irresponsible and buffoon-like Bob was, and that he couldn't represent Alaska as well as Uncle Vic. But for some reason, the result was just the opposite and struck a chord with the people of Alaska—a good chord, at that.

***

Election day finally came and Bob was still considering his chances nil to slight. The best thing that would come out of this is just more fodder for his comic routines. Other than that, he wasn't too concerned with the election results. Uncle Vic would win by a landslide, just like he's done so many times before.

After voting early, he went over to The Whale's Tail to see the pretty blond bartender. He hoped to work up the courage to ask her out one day. He would love to show her his hometown of Nome. He walked into the lounge even though it wasn't open yet. There she was, working behind the bar and talking with a woman Bob later learned was a good friend Jane. She poured him a coffee and asked if he voted yet.

Bob replied, "Yes." She asked him who he voted for with that smile of hers. Bob just mumbled, "I don't remember."

She smiled and asked when he was going over to Bernie's lounge to watch the returns come in.

He replied, "I don't know, maybe later."

She said she would be there when she got off shift. At that, Bob decided to be there also.

His next stop was at the Cabin Tavern. Might as well make the rounds, he thought. After entering, he was waiting for his eyes to adjust and he heard Tiny call out, "Hey Bobby! Or should I say Mr. Congressman elect?"

"Ah, no, no, that will never happen. This whole running for Congress has gotten a little, ah, a little, overblown," he answered as his eyes adjusted and he saw bartender Karen, Dave, and regular Jon at the bar.

He walked to the bar and took his usual stool. Dave slapped him on the back and said he voted for him. Jon gave him the *Star Trek* Vulcan live long and prosper sign.

Karen simply said, "Well, Bucko, what'll it be, Mr. Congressman elect? You know, when you get to Washington, you're going to have to start drinking some upper-shelf alcohol. Maybe even wine!"

At that, Dave chimed in, "Wine, it's how classy people get sh*tfaced."

And Tiny just sat there at his puzzle with that knowing grin of his.

# Chapter 10 — Mr. Congressman

Come mid-afternoon, and Bob finally wandered over to Bernie's lounge. Although it was the beginning of November, it appeared as if they would have a late winter. All one needed was a light jacket to be comfortable outside. There was termination dust on the Chugach Mountains, but only halfway down. Termination dust is the first snow on the mountains marking the termination of summer. Again he was met by Bernie with that friendly smile of his.

"What'll be the Congressman's pleasure?" Bernie asked.

Bob thought, then said, "It's, it's a little early for Mr. Congressman, but not too early for an Irish whiskey!" Bob received his Irish and started to mingle with the early crowd. After all, it was sort of free advertisement for his comedy shows. As the day moved into late afternoon, the crowd grew. The Governor was present, talking with a few important-looking people.

The first early returns came over the television screens Bernie had set up around the outside gathering area. The numbers were no surprise to Bob, and by now, he didn't even pay attention to the screens. With 20 percent of the precincts reporting, Uncle Vic was ahead by 96%. As the day moved into the evening, the crowd grew. The pretty blond bartender arrived. Tiny and Karen were seen at one table and Tiny raised his glass to toast Bob. Bernie made the rounds of the various tables playing host and made sure Bob was introduced to more people than he could remember.

The evening went on and now the returns with 50% of the precincts reporting had Bob and Uncle Vic neck and neck. A cheer went up when those numbers made their appearance on the screens. But Bob wasn't paying much attention; maybe it was the Irish whiskey or the pretty blond bartender. Bob was with her at one of the tables with no one else around. The clammer and noise seemed to melt away and Bob had all his attention on her. He was trying to keep the Irish whiskey from showing as he spoke.

"Ah, I...I saw your...your truck the other day. Your license plate has KANOE on it. Why, ah, do you have Kanoe on your license plate? Did someone already have CANOE?"

She just smiled and said, "For someone running for Congress, you're still a little naive. That's my Hawaiian name. It's short for Kanoelani. If you ever get to Hawaii and look up to the Ko'olau Mountains, the mist you might see is called heavenly mist."

Bob nodded and realized the pretty blond bartender, or Kanoe, was actually explaining this to him without calling him a haole man. "Ah, um. Should I call you Kanoe?"

She replied, "I was wondering how long it was going to take for you to ask. Actually, no. My first name is Ruby. Ruby will be fine," she said with a warm smile.

"So, ah, so...maybe after all this, this ridiculous election goes away, would, would, you like to come visit Nome? It's a beautiful place. I, I, could get you a discount room at the Nugget Inn."

"Hey haole man, so you think I'm only worth a cheap, fleabag discount inn?" she replied.

"Ah, ah, ah, no, no, that's, that's not what I meant," Bob tried to explain.

Of course, Bob didn't see the slight smile on Ruby's face. He explained it would be a very nice room, one of the best in the inn. He would make sure of that. Bob had been thinking of a trip like this for a long time. He wanted to show her Nome, the Board of Trade, panning for gold on the beach, the Bima gold dredge, the musk ox and caribou roaming the tundra. Oh, Bob had big plans.

And she just smiled and said, "Bob, let's wait and see." With that, she got up and patted Bob's hand and said she had to go as she had an early shift tomorrow.

And Bob felt as if he was walking on air. He now knew Ruby's name and she actually started to call him Bob.

Another cheer went up from the crowd and Bob was still oblivious. He didn't remember much of what happened after that except Aunt Mary and Albert helping him home and putting him to bed.

***


Bob slept in the next day. It wasn't until late morning that he became conscious, conscious of a throbbing headache. Albert came in and gave him a drink with that toothy smile of his. Bob wasn't in the mood to drink anything, but Albert just explained it was Aunt Mary's medicine for celebrating too much the night before. Bob questioned his nephew's words, but he smelled Aunt Mary's cooking and waved Albert off. He heard Aunt Mary humming to herself in the kitchen and made his way to the dining area with Albert following.

"So dear, or should I say Mr. Congressman elect, how are you feeling?" she asked.

Bob wasn't in the mood to answer any more Congressman jabs and just said okay and dove into breakfast. Aunt Mary and Albert just grinned at each other. Then Aunt Mary told Albert to put on the television, which he did, and found a news channel reporting on the election. Bob was only half paying attention until he saw the return numbers. With 93% of the precincts reporting, Bob was ahead by 82%.

"Wha...what just happened?" Bob managed to choke out a mouthful of pancakes, "is this some type of joke?"

Aunt Mary and Albert smiled at him and just said, "No, Mr. Congressman elect, you took the election!"

While Bob finished his breakfast and was sipping his coffee, he mumbled there must be a mistake. He didn't know how to be a Congressman. Aunt Mary assured him he would be fine with that twinkle in her eye. She said he would have plenty of help, the Governor would always be available to consult with, and he could keep Uncle Vic's staff.

Uncle Vic finally conceded, and the congratulatory phone calls started to come in. The following day he received telegrams from Greenland on his victory. What was even more surprising, he received a few from Denmark. What Bob didn't know was that his nephew Albert had covered his uncle's victory and posted it on their YouTube channel. But Denmark?

"Why in the world would I get telegrams from Denmark?" Bob mused over his coffee.

"Ah, well, Uncle," Albert began, "remember that DNA test I had you do a while back?"

"Albert, yes, but what does that have to do with anything?" Bob asked between sips of his coffee.

"Well, Uncle, remember when I told you your paternal family line was one of the last waves of people migrating to Europe?" Albert continued.

"Go on," Bob replied.

And Albert continued, "Well, it seems your family passed through the area where Denmark is today on their way to what today is now Normandy."

"Go on." Bob was mildly interested.

"Well, I sort of added your family odyssey to our YouTube channel. I thought it might make you more interesting and get us more subscribers," Albert explained. "And it seems to have worked, Uncle. You now have a small following in Denmark in addition to Greenland!"

***

The next several weeks, Bob made the rounds and thanked all his supporters. He was still half-dazed about what happened. But he figured that he would run his one term and retire from this unforeseen political adventure. And he thought he'd just collect more material for his comedy routine. What better place than Congress to do that?

He visited Ruby and was successful in his invitation to show her Nome. They had a beautiful long weekend in Nome and even found quite a bit of gold on the beach. She particularly enjoyed the dog sled ride.

He spent quite a bit of time in the Governor's office discussing Alaska's needs and country and world events.

Bob made it to the Cabin Tavern to thank Tiny and bartender Karen. When he arrived, he paused for a moment to let his eyes adjust to the dim interior. At least it was dim compared to the bright sun outside.

"Hey, bucko, nice of you to remember us now that you're a big shot, Congressman," Karen called from behind the bar.

"Well, ah, it, ah, not really, Congressman yet," Bob replied.

As his eyes adjusted, he saw Dave at the bar with his after-shift beer.

Bob went on to say maybe he should learn how to drink wine now that he was heading to the lower 48. Karen asked what type he preferred, and Bob replied red, as that was supposed to be healthier. After some more prodding from Karen and Dave, Bob indicated that he was interested in something with a full-bodied taste and an earthy aroma. Karen poured him a glass of red zinfandel and held the glass up in front of Bob. She explained that a full-body wine would leave legs on the side of the glass after swirling the glass. Bob sipped the wine and was surprised at how smooth it was with that earthy aroma he liked. He finished his glass and a few more before bidding farewell, but he would be back before he left for Washington.

***

The next few weeks were busy for Bob, Aunt Mary, and nephew Albert. Not that they had a lot of household goods to ship to Washington, D.C., but the logistics kept them all busy.

Bob did have time to visit the local liquor store and purchase some zinfandel. He bought a box of their finest.

Before leaving Anchorage, he did manage to make one more visit to the Cabin Tavern.

It was mid-afternoon when he walked into the Cabin. Before his eyes adjusted, he made his way over to his spot on the bar. He didn't yet see Tiny working his crossword puzzle at the end of the bar. He didn't even see the two ladies a couple of seats to either side of Bob's favorite stool. He probably wishes he did, but it probably wouldn't have made any difference. They were both redheads with long, deep red hair. One was dressed in a form-fitting light, black sweater, short black skirt, and black stockings showing off long, graceful legs. The other was similarly dressed but in red and white.

Bob stopped a few feet from his stool and, as his eyes adjusted, saw Karen with that questioning look as if to say, 'What do you want, bucko?'

Without hesitation and hoping to show off his newfound expertise with wine, he simply said, "Something red, with legs, and smells like dirt!"

He didn't see both ladies suddenly straighten their backs, Karen stepping back, or that grin playing on Tiny's face. He simply moved up to the bar, then noticed the ladies. He turned to acknowledge the lady to his left.

SLAP! Bob recoiled to his right. SPLASH! And the two ladies got up and left the bar. Karen just shook her head.

Tiny just said, "Bobby, Bobby, Bobby. You still have a way with women, and your timing is still impeccable."

***

Soon January came, and Bob headed to Washington, D.C., to be sworn in as the "Congressman for all Alaska." The Governor was in attendance, as were Aunt Mary and Albert. Bob had protested about having Albert there as he had his schooling to attend in Nome. However, Aunt Mary had arranged for him to enroll in school in Washington. She thought living in the Capital would be a great experience for Albert and would broaden his experience. And Aunt Mary was there to keep an eye on him...and on Bob.

They found an apartment to lease not too far from the Capital. Bob attended Congress 101 and was soon deeply involved in Congress with the help of occasional encouragement and tips from the Governor.

# Chapter 11 — Mr. Speaker

Washington D.C., Georgetown, at the Seasons Restaurant, the Arbor Room had been booked a week in advance. Among the diners were the Speaker of the House and two ranking Congressmen from both sides of the aisle. A total of five men were present to eat, drink, and discuss the future of the House of Representatives. A closed meeting might not have been the best venue for discussing government business. The atmosphere was reminiscent of smoke-filled backroom politics.

After the food was served and drinks arrived, the Speaker instructed the manager that they were not to be disturbed. They would notify the management when something was required.

The Speaker started the discussion about the business at hand. "As you all know, my health has not been good as of late. Unfortunately, I will have to resign as Speaker but plan on staying on as a representative. The situation of the House currently has an even split between our two parties, with one independent, that country bumpkin from Alaska."

Discussion followed among the little group as to who should be the next Speaker. No one wanted the job. With mid-term elections a year away, each Congressman was more concerned with their re-election than the business of the House. Between the recently elected President and the inaction in the House, whatever party the new Speaker was from would no doubt be a public relations nightmare for their party.

"What about that bumpkin from Alaska?" asked one of the Congressmen, "it won't matter how much he screws up. He probably won't be re-elected anyway. He's an independent and still a green freshman at that. We can then all concentrate on our mid-terms and may the best party win."

More discussion and more drinks followed. The more the idea was discussed, the better it sounded.

"Well, if we're going to do this, we have to make sure he is willing to accept the position," the Speaker explained, "we'll have to blow a hell of a lot of smoke up his skirt as to how the country needs him, and lay on a guilt trip if he hesitates."

They decided they could convince the "Congressman for all Alaska" to accept the position of Speaker of the House. After all, it was only for one more year. They also thought it would be very easy to manipulate Bob in their favor.

So the plan went into play with visits from each of the senior Congressmen to Bob's office. This culminated in another reservation at the Arbor Room, except this time, Bob was invited. Bob was a little in awe at dining with these senior Congressmen and in a private room at that. He felt he didn't quite fit in and felt like a moose in the headlights. He quickly came back to reality and gave his order to the server. Although he was going to show off his newfound wine education, he noticed all the men were drinking brown liquor and quickly changed his mind. He ordered his Irish whiskey.

The senior Congressmen outlined their need for an impartial Speaker and Bob was the man for the job. It would be a great honor for both him and Alaska. Bob asked for a little time to think it over and totally missed the glances the Congressmen gave each other.

***

After the meeting at the Arbor Room, Bob returned home to his apartment. Aunt Mary was there, but Albert was still at school. Now Aunt Mary had made herself indispensable to Bob's Congressional office. She essentially became his Chief of Staff. Somehow, she totally integrated herself into Congress and seemed to know exactly what was happening and why. She also developed a keen sense of international politics. How did this happen? Bob couldn't even guess.

Bob explained what had happened and that he was asked to be Speaker of the House. Aunt Mary listened intently like she always did with that knowing smile of hers.

After Bob was finished, Aunt Mary simply said, "Well, dear, those men may not have had your best interest at heart or the best interest of the country. But that doesn't mean you shouldn't consider the opportunity. Think about it."

Albert soon returned from his after-school activities, and the three of them enjoyed another of Aunt Mary's dinners.

A couple of days later, Bob contacted the Speaker and said he would be honored to accept the position. The Speaker said there would be some formalities to go through, but not to worry; the entire Congress would be behind him.

***

It was a beautiful day when Bob was sworn in as the Speaker of the House. Albert was there with his video camera, collecting clips for his YouTube channel. Aunt Mary was also there in her native parka, with a big grin on her face. Bob was surprised to see the Governor in attendance but was relieved he was there.

As the weeks wore on, Speaker Bob realized just how dysfunctional the House had become. It was just about impossible to get any business done. The members seemed to spend all their time arguing and sniping at each other. That is, when they were there and not out campaigning or enjoying free lunches from lobbyists.

# Chapter 12 - Mr. President Dear

It was late at night, and the lights burned low in the Oval Office. The President was pacing the room as the Vice President continued, "There has been some disturbing information that some journalist dug up. It has to do with your hotel deals in Russia. I'm afraid it will be all over the press in a few days. In addition to that, there's some scuttlebutt about you using the CIA to obtain information so you could use it as blackmail on these deals."

The Attorney General was present and agreed with the Vice President.

The President, obviously agitated, responded, "It'll blow over. No need to worry. I'm the damn President! They can't touch me!"

***

Well, the President was indeed touched. And the press had a field day. All this led to another late night in the Oval Office. This time it was only the President and Vice President.

"Idiots, idiots. That's all they are!" ranted the President. "They can't get rid of me! There has to be a way around this!"

The President came up with a workable solution, so he thought. The plan was for him to resign. This would make the Vice President move into the President's position. Then all he would have to do is pardon the then-former President. Sounded simple enough. However, the Vice President had no desire to become the President. More brainstorming into the night. Then the two reached a workaround compromise.

The President will resign. The Vice President will become President and pardon the then-former President. As his Vice President, the "new" President will pick the former President. The new President will resign. And the original President is back in power with a pardon. What could go wrong?

***

So the day arrived to put the scheme into action. The press was invited, and members of Congress were invited, including the Speaker of the House, Bob. All with no explanation of any announcement from the White House. The President was waiting to go to the podium, but there was a hitch. No one knew where the Vice President was. Members of Congress were present. The press was in attendance. No Vice President. The White House staff finally found him, and he was on the way to the White House from a business meeting.

The crowd was beginning to get a little loud and annoyed. The day was exceptionally warm, and everyone, including the President, was anxious to get things moving. After being assured that the Vice President would be here shortly, the President made his way to the podium.

***

A little earlier in the day, the Vice President and his Secret Service contingent left for his business meeting. As he entered his official state car, the suspension groaned, and the car sank a bit.

The driver rolled his eyes and said quietly to one of the Secret Service officers, "One would think he would watch his weight a little better."

Off the contingent drove to the business meeting. Actually, it was a business lunch with a journalist. Even though the Vice President had a large American breakfast with ham, eggs, potatoes, French toast, coffee, and juice, he managed to consume a very large lunch. One of the Secret Service officers commented that the only reason the VP went on the business lunch was for the lunch.

The lunch, er, business meeting came to a close, and the contingent saddled up for the return trip to the White House. They were on schedule to make the President's formal announcement. However, halfway back, the VP instructed the driver to go through the drive-through of a local fast-food restaurant.

# THE RELUCTANT PRESIDENT, BELLWETHER BOB

"But sir, you just had lunch with that lady journalist, and we have a schedule..." the driver said weakly.

"I did not have lunch with that woman," admonished the VP in his hoarse Arkansas accent while he pointed a finger at the driver.

"Yes, sir!" responded the driver as he pulled into the drive-through.

"Not again!" one of the Secret Service officers said to his coworker in the accompanying car. "He does this almost all the time!"

***

"Effectively immediately, I resign as the President of the United States!" the President said at the podium at the White House.

Well, the crowd wasn't expecting this announcement. Many thought the President would put up an amusing fight. The President had a smirk on his face as he stepped back to await the arrival of the VP.

***

"The VPOTUS is down! I repeat, VPOTUS is down!" The Secret Service's radio communication to the White House kept repeating.

A massive heart attack left the VP dead at the scene. Unfortunately, the lavish and excessive meals finally caught up with the VP.

The news was leaked at the White House, and both Congressional representatives and members of the press all started talking at once. Then there was silence, and everyone turned and looked at Bob.

The Speaker of the House was third in line for the Presidency. And Bob was sworn in that day as President.

The VP laid in state the following week in a super-sized coffin. The former President disappeared and was rumored to be living in Russia and was never heard of again.

Bob needed a Vice President and chose Aunt Mary. However, he had to request Aunt Mary not call him "dear" while in public or in the White House. At which she just gave him that smile of hers.

Both political parties appeared to heartily endorse Bob as the President. What Bob did not know was each was scheming to take credit for anything good he did and blame him for any failures.

# Chapter 13 — What Just Happened?

To say the next few weeks were a whirlwind of moving, debriefings, relocation, congratulations, interviews, and numbness for Bob was an understatement. However, with VPOTUS Aunt Mary and nephew Albert, Bob managed to hold it together.

***

Not too long after Bob was sworn into office, Greenland and Denmark requested a visit from a high-ranking government official. Bob was going to assign the Secretary of State with this request. However, Aunt Mary convinced Bob it would be better if she attended to the matter. So Aunt Mary left for the state visit and, of course, brought Albert with her.

Aunt Mary and nephew Albert went on their state trip and Albert was ecstatic to see both Greenland and Denmark. On their return to Washington, they debriefed Bob. It seemed that Greenland and Denmark wanted to form closer ties with the United States and, after the groundwork was roughed out with Aunt Mary, would like to meet with President Bob.

Bob tried to learn all he could about Greenland and Denmark to include joint operations and cooperation. He requested that the Secretary of Defense come to the White House to confer on the issue.

***

The next week, Bob was in the Oval Office when the Secretary of Defense arrived for their meeting.

Aunt Mary escorted the Secretary, and she opened the door to the Oval Office and peeked in. Bob was nowhere in sight.

"Oh, Mr. President, dear," she called out.

At that, she heard a loud thump under the Resolute Desk. Bob rose up from behind the desk, rubbing his head.

"What are you doing, dear?" asked Aunt Mary.

"Um, ah, I just thought I saw some carving under the, ah, desk," explained Bob.

"Well, never mind that, dear. Mr. Secretary of Defense is here to see you," Aunt Mary explained.

So the Secretary of Defense went into the Oval Office, followed by Aunt Mary. A little small talk ensued, and then Aunt Mary debriefed the Secretary on her trip to Greenland and Denmark.

The Secretary thought for a moment and responded that close cooperation with both Greenland and Denmark was always a priority. He recommended that the meeting take place at the Thule Air Base. Aunt Mary left to have the staff start on the preparations for the trip. This left just Bob and the Secretary in the room. As the conversation left the topic of the trip, Bob mused that he had always wanted to ride on a nuclear-powered submarine.

"Well, Mr. President," the Secretary continued, "you are the Commander-in-Chief."

"You, you mean I could ride on a submarine?" Bob sort of stammered out. "I don't want to inconvenience the Navy or anything."

The Secretary of Defense smiled and assured Bob that it could be arranged for a short trip into port. There is one due in a couple of weeks, and he'll make the arrangements.

Bob was elated like a little boy going on his first boat ride.

"Oh, and Mr. President, they are good people in both Greenland and Denmark. They'll treat you right," called out the Secretary on his way out of the Oval Office.

***

So Bob, Aunt Mary, nephew Albert, and their support staff went on to Greenland.

Upon arriving at Thule Air Base, they settled into their quarters. Bob was briefed by the Base Commander, and they prepared for the next day's meeting. The meeting was to be attended by the Premier of Greenland and the Prime Minister of Denmark.

***

While Bob thought this was just a type of "meet and greet" get-together, he was a little surprised as the meeting progressed. The meeting wasn't largely attended as the support staffs were kept to a minimum. However, Bob caught a glimpse of some of the support staff from Greenland and Denmark wearing the "...and that's why the walrus crossed the road" shirts that nephew Albert had sold on his YouTube channel.

While Bob was extensively briefed by his Department of State and Secretary of Defense on all things related to Greenland before leaving the White House, he found it a little hard to keep up with what was being proposed.

It seems both Greenland and Denmark had an amiable disposition towards Bob. The meeting progressed more like some old friends getting together rather than Heads of State.

The bottom line, from what Bob could tell, is that the people of Greenland would love to become part of the United States. Bob glanced at Aunt Mary, and she had a look on her face as if she wasn't surprised. Denmark was in agreement with the arrangement, but there was a catch. It seemed Denmark was having a slight cash problem, and they floated a dollar figure for compensation. Bob knew how important Greenland was but was taken aback by this dollar figure.

After much discussion, the group broke up for lunch. Bob took this opportunity to make a secure phone call to the Secretary of State and the Secretary of Defense. A counter-proposal was discussed, and everyone knew such a deal would require Congressional approval.

After lunch, Bob made his counter-proposal to the group. If the United States agreed to the price, would Denmark consider spending a percentage of that money purchasing United States goods? A silence descended on the meeting. The Premier and the Prime Minister requested a timeout while they conferred with their governments. Upon returning, the smiles on their faces indicated a deal was near.

The next day, each country's officials and staff departed Thule to confer with their respective governments with a plan to complete a telephonic update within a month.

***

After meetings with both the Senate and the House of Representatives, Bob was pleasantly surprised by their receptiveness to the whole idea. Little did he realize it was just politics being played out. Both political parties saw this as an opportunity to claim credit if this whole idea of purchasing Greenland succeeded and to deflect all blame back to Bob if it fell flat. And Aunt Mary just kept that knowing smile of hers as the process worked its way through the machinations of government.

So one day, the United States was about 840,000 square miles larger as Greenland became a territory of the United States. Public support for Greenland was even stronger than Bob and the legislature imagined. It was so amazing that within two months, Greenland went from a territory to the 51st state in the Union! Heads were definitely spinning. Now Alaska was the second largest state in the Union, and Texas now the third.

One day Bob went into the Oval Office and found Aunt Mary waiting for him. She held up a United States flag which looked a little different to Bob. It took Bob a while to realize that the flag had 51 stars on it. Later that day, as Bob left the White House, he noticed the same flag flying high. It seems Greenland was definitely welcomed with open arms by the country.

# Chapter 14 — A Cat for a Hat

After the exuberance of welcoming Greenland into the Union, the Secretary of Defense came to see Bob.

"Do you still want to ride on a submarine, Mr. President?" the Secretary asked Bob.

Bob's eyes lit up like a little kid's. "You bet I do! Is that possible?"

"Well, Mr. President, we have a sub coming in next week and we can make arrangements if you have a couple of days..."

Bob interrupted the Secretary mid-sentence, "If I have a couple of days? Of course, I do. Just have some meetings with Congress. But I'll reschedule those. Priorities! Oh, I also have a meeting with the Queen of Denmark, but I'm sure she'll understand."

So it was set and Bob flew out to the incoming sub on a military helicopter. Once on board, he was given a VIP tour and treatment by the Captain.

After the tour, Bob and the Captain were making small talk and the Captain informed Bob they would be making port a little after sundown. The Captain also thanked Bob for his part in enabling Greenland to be our 51st state. Bob thought it a little odd that the Captain spoke with a slight Scottish accent but paid it no mind.

As sunset grew near, the Captain and Bob were on the conning tower. The sub passed a river on the way to port and Bob commented that his father taught him to fish in a similar river. The evening air was a bit chilly and Bob forgot to pack a hat. The Captain called down and soon, an ensign appeared with a black lambswool hat for Bob. Bob thanked the Captain and the ensign and put on the hat.

"Hmmm", said Bob, "what's that purring noise I hear?"

The Captain replied it was their new engine that was installed in the sub. It really increased their speed and stealth.

***

"Oh gosh, look at Uncle! It looks like he was out on the deck all night. The mosquito bites!" exclaimed the older sister.

"Oh no," said the other sister, "it looks like he got into our brownies! Look, you get rid of the brownies and I'll wake up Uncle Bob. He must have come back early from his Talkeetna trip!"

The other sister questioned, "What is that on his head? Oh, it's that fat feral cat, and it's purring up a storm."

As the sisters approached Uncle Bob, the fat cat jumped off and walked over to the side of the deck. One sister collected up the brownies or what remained of them.

The other sister gently shook her uncle. "Uncle, Uncle, are you okay? It looks like you had a rough night."

Bob was pretty groggy and it took him a while to fully wake up.

"Where, where am I? Why, why are you on the submarine? Where's the Captain? Where's my hat?" Bob stammered out.

"No, I don't know what you're talking about, Uncle. It looks like you fell asleep on the deck last night," explained one sister.

"No, it's...it...can't be," Bob said as he began waking up fully. "Wait! How many stars are on our flag?"

"Uncle, don't be silly. There are 50 stars on the flag."

The sisters helped Bob get up and move into the little house, put lotion on his mosquito bites, and fixed him some strong coffee. As they chatted, Bob relayed how he came back early from his Talkeetna trip due to not feeling well. That he took some type of home remedy and sat down on the deck and must have dosed off and had this dream that was so lifelike. The sisters glanced at each other with a sigh of relief.

"Well, Uncle, why don't you come over to our place and have dinner with us? I'm sure Mom and Dad would be interested in hearing about your Talkeetna trip and that dream of yours."

# Epilogue

Things eventually got back to normal, and Bob worked his way back into his pre-Talkeetna trip routine. Although he had to check with Aunt Mary and nephew Albert just to make sure he was back to reality, covertly, of course.

The months passed, and nothing earth-shaking occurred. The fat feral cat still kept Bob company. His nieces kept an eye on their uncle just to make sure there were no "side effects."

Life was pretty uneventful for Bob. He made his weekly trips to the Cabin Tavern, fed the feral cats much to the consternation of his landlord, Jed, and visited with Ruby at the Whale's Tail Lounge.

Then in May, Bob won the Nenana Ice Classic by guessing the time to the minute and the date the ice went out on the Tanana River. As he was the only one that guessed that particular date and time, he pocketed a nice $230,000, before taxes, of course. Thinking he deserved a little relaxation and remembering Ruby's advice, he booked a trip to Hawaii. As he had the time and now the funds, Bob decided to take a cruise to Hawaii. What could go wrong on a nice, easy, relaxing cruise to Hawaii?

***

"So what's your brother going to do now that he's rich?" Bill asked his wife, Felicitas.

"He decided to take a cruise to Hawaii," replied Felicitas.

"Nice. What ship did he book?" asked Bill, as he was familiar with the shipping and cruise industry.

"Oh, I think it was the *Ajax*," answered Felicitas.

Bill thought for a moment and replied, "Hmm...I don't recall any cruise ship by that name..."

What could go wrong?